THE BIG BOOK OF
THE ALOLA REGION

ISBN 978-1-5247-7009-9

randomhousekids.com

Printed in the United States of America

10 9 8 7 6 5 4 3 2 1

The Alolan islands are inhabited by very special creatures known as Pokémon. A boy named Ash Ketchum and his best friend, a Pokémon called Pikachu, are new to the area. Ash joins a group of skilled young Trainers—Kiawe, Lana, Mallow, and Sophocles—along with the cool Professor Kukui and Samson Oak to learn all about this region's Pokémon.

PIKACHU ⚡

Height: 1'04" / **Weight:** 13.2 lbs.
Type: Electric
Category: Mouse Pokémon

Ash has come to Alola from Pallet Town in the Kanto region with his best friend and loyal companion **Pikachu**, an Electric-type Pokémon. Ash dreams of one day becoming a true Pokémon Master, and Alola offers a variety of exciting new Pokémon to discover!

Rowlet, Litten, and Popplio are just a few of the newly discovered Pokémon from the Alola region.

ROWLET

Height: 1'00" / Weight: 3.3 lbs.
Type: Grass-Flying
Category: Grass Quill Pokémon

Rowlet is a Grass- and Flying-type Pokémon that stores energy from the sun during the day and becomes active at night. It can fly and attack without making a sound!

LITTEN

Height: 1'04" / Weight: 9.5 lbs.
Type: Fire
Category: Fire Cat Pokémon

Litten is a cool-headed Fire-type Pokémon that takes a while to warm up to strangers. It attacks with flaming hairballs!

POPPLIO

Height: 1'04" / Weight: 16.5 lbs.
Type: Water
Category: Sea Lion Pokémon

Popplio is a hardworking Water-type Pokémon that smashes its foes with bubbles!

KOMALA ⊙

Height: 1'04" / Weight: 43.9 lbs.
Type: Normal
Category: Drowsing Pokémon

Komala sleeps day and night, but it sometimes moves around as it dreams, cuddling its log. If it can't find its log, it's been known to cling to a friendly Trainer's arm.

YUNGOOS ⊙

Height: 1'04" / Weight: 13.2 lbs.
Type: Normal
Category: Loitering Pokémon

Yungoos spends its days looking for food, which it chomps with its powerful teeth. It is not picky when it comes to meals or sleep— when night falls, it immediately passes out wherever it happens to be.

Eevee and Munchlax are native to other regions but can also be found in Alola.

EEVEE ⊙

Height: 1'00" / **Weight:** 14.3 lbs.
Type: Normal
Category: Evolution Pokémon

Eevee is both adorable and adaptive: according to current studies, it can evolve into eight different Pokémon!

MUNCHLAX ⊙

Height: 2'00" / **Weight:** 231.5 lbs.
Type: Normal
Category: Big Eater Pokémon

Munchlax needs to consume its own weight in food every day, so it eats anything that looks edible, no matter the taste! Munchlax evolves into Snorlax.

PIKIPEK ◯ ☾
Height: 1'00" / Weight: 2.6 lbs.
Type: Normal-Flying
Category: Woodpecker Pokémon

TRUMBEAK ◯ ☾
Height: 2'00" / Weight: 32.6 lbs.
Type: Normal-Flying
Category: Bugle Beak Pokémon

Pikipek is a Flying-type Pokémon that feeds on berries and uses its sturdy beak to drill holes in trees. It uses these holes as both a nest and a place to store berries.

TOUCANNON ◯ ☾
Height: 3'07" / Weight: 57.3 lbs.
Type: Normal-Flying
Category: Cannon Pokémon

Pikipek evolves into Trumbeak, and then into Toucannon. **Trumbeak** can bend its beak to produce a variety of noisy sounds. **Toucannon's** beak reaches temperatures over 200 degrees Fahrenheit, allowing it to launch seeds that can cause serious burns!

TURTONATOR 🔥 🐉

Height: 6'07" / Weight: 467.4 lbs.
Type: Fire-Dragon
Category: Blast Turtle Pokémon

Turtonator is an intimidating Fire- and Dragon-type Pokémon native to Alola. It gushes flames and fumes from its nostrils. Its shell can explode when hit!

ALOLAN MAROWAK 🔥 👻

Height: 3'03" / Weight: 75.0 lbs.
Type: Fire-Ghost
Category: Bone Keeper Pokémon

Alolan Marowak is a Fire- and Ghost-type Pokémon, unlike the Ground-type Marowak first found in the Kanto region. The flaming bone it grasps once belonged to its mother, and it is protected by its mother's spirit.

Certain Pokémon from other regions have adapted to their Alolan habitat, resulting in different types and appearances!

Oricorio is one of the most unique Pokémon in Alola. By consuming different nectars on the four islands, it can change its style and type.

ORICORIO
Height: 2'00" / Weight: 7.5 lbs.
Category: Dancing Pokémon

BAILE STYLE 🔥 🌙
Type: Fire-Flying

Oricorio's **Baile Style** passionately beats its wings together to produce intense flames, so this display is best observed from a distance!

PA'U STYLE ◉ 🌙
Type: Psychic-Flying

Pa'u Style Oricorio hypnotizes its opponent with calm, gentle swaying—before attacking with psychic energy!

POM-POM STYLE ⚡ 🌙
Type: Electric-Flying

In **Pom-Pom Style**, Oricorio's bright, cheerful dance generates an electric charge to zap its enemies.

SENSU STYLE 👻 🌙
Type: Ghost-Flying

While in its **Sensu Style**, Oricorio elegantly summons the spirits of the departed and uses their energy to curse enemies.

Magikarp is known for lacking battle strength. When attacked, Magikarp splashes about recklessly, and its attacks are extremely ineffective to its opponents. While Magikarp may perform poorly in battle, they exist in huge numbers.

MAGIKARP

Height: 2'11" / **Weight:** 22.0 lbs.
Type: Water
Category: Fish Pokémon

GYARADOS

Height: 21'04" / **Weight:** 518.1 lbs.
Type: Water-Flying
Category: Atrocious Pokémon

When Magikarp evolves, it leaves its weakness behind to become a mighty **Gyarados**! Gyarados possesses an infamous temper and will destroy everything in its path once it becomes enraged.

Gyarados's power and strength can level entire towns—especially if it Mega Evolves into the Water- and Dark-type Mega Gyarados!

BRUXISH

Height: 2'11" / **Weight:** 41.9 lbs.
Type: Water-Psychic
Category: Gnash Teeth Pokémon

Bruxish uses the flowerlike bulb on its head to unleash powerful psychic blasts and stun its opponents. The grinding of its massive teeth is powerful enough to crunch through the hardest shells!

PYUKUMUKU

Height: 1'00" / **Weight:** 2.6 lbs.
Type: Water
Category: Sea Cucumber Pokémon

Pyukumuku is a small water-dwelling Pokémon that lives in shallow seas near beaches, and the sticky slime that covers its body can be used to soothe sunburned skin. In battle, Pyukumuku can eject its internal organs to damage enemies—eww!

BOUNSWEET

Height: 1'00" / **Weight:** 7.1 lbs.
Type: Grass
Category: Fruit Pokémon

Bounsweet releases a delectable aroma, and the sugary liquid it gives off can be watered down into a tasty sweet treat.

EXEGGUTOR

Height: 6'07" / **Weight:** 264.6 lbs.
Type: Grass-Psychic
Category: Coconut Pokémon

Exeggutor are found in regions other than Alola, but they are rather different in appearance from Alolan Exeggutor! Exeggutor's three heads each have a mind of their own, and any decision made is discussed by all three!

ALOLAN EXEGGUTOR

Height: 35'09" / **Weight:** 916.2 lbs.
Type: Grass-Dragon
Category: Coconut Pokémon

Something about the island climate clearly agrees with Exeggutor. **Alolan Exeggutor** grew taller, and taller, and taller, and eventually outgrew its reliance on psychic abilities. Instead, the power of the dragon awoke from deep within Alolan Exeggutor!

ALOLAN RAICHU ⚡ ◐

Height: 2'04" / **Weight:** 46.3 lbs.
Type: Electric-Psychic
Category: Mouse Pokémon

Pikachu evolves into Raichu, and **Alolan Raichu** is an Electric-Psychic type that can use its tail like a surfboard. Researchers think Raichu looks different in the Alola region because of what it eats.

TOGEDEMARU ⚡ ⬡

Height: 1'00" / **Weight:** 7.3 lbs.
Type: Electric-Steel
Category: Roly-Poly Pokémon

Togedemaru is the Roly-Poly Pokémon. When Togedemaru is at rest, its fur is soft and smooth—but when agitated or threatened, its lightning-conducting spines stand up to ward off attacks!

Tapu Koko is a mysterious and powerful guardian deity Pokémon of the island of Melemele. It stores lightning in its body to unleash devastating attacks!

ALOLAN VULPIX ❄

Height: 2'00" / Weight: 21.8 lbs.
Type: Ice
Category: Fox Pokémon

The adorable **Alolan Vulpix** has adapted to the cold climate of Alola's mountain peaks and, unlike previously discovered Vulpix, is an Ice type, not a Fire-type Pokémon! When Alolan Vulpix becomes too hot, it creates ice shards with its six tails to stay cool.

ALOLAN ❄ ❜❜
NINETALES

Height: 3'07" / Weight: 43.9 lbs.
Type: Ice-Fairy
Category: Fox Pokémon

Alolan Vulpix evolves into the beautiful **Alolan Ninetales**. It is a cool and collected Pokémon, until it becomes angry and freezes its enemy in its tracks! Its dual Ice and Fairy types make it particularly menacing to Dragon-type Pokémon.

Like Alolan Vulpix, **Alolan Sandshrew** has adapted to the wintry temperatures of Alola's mountains. Unlike the Ground-type Sandshrew found in other regions, Alolan Sandshrew are Ice- and Steel-type.

ALOLAN SANDSHREW ❄ ⬡

Height: 2'04" / **Weight:** 88.2 lbs.
Type: Ice-Steel
Category: Mouse Pokémon

GLALIE ❄

Height: 4'11" / **Weight:** 565.5 lbs.
Type: Ice
Category: Face Pokémon

Myths say that **Glalie** came into being when a rock on a snowy peak soaked up the despair of a lost traveler. Now it uses the icy air from its giant mouth to freeze its opponents solid!

CRABRAWLER

Height: 2'00" / **Weight:** 15.4 lbs.
Type: Fighting
Category: Boxing Pokémon

Crabrawler punches so furiously that sometimes its claws fall off—but thankfully, they grow back quickly! This Fighting-type Pokémon really hates to lose.

LUCARIO

Height: 3'11" / **Weight:** 119.0 lbs.
Type: Fighting-Steel
Category: Aura Pokémon

Lucario is the evolved form of Riolu. It has trained hard enough to identify and control auras and use them in battle for powerful attacks. It is said that Lucario is able to Mega Evolve!

Looks can be deceiving: **Stufful** may seem harmless and cuddly, but when it gets angry, its flailing arms and legs can send Trainers and Pokémon alike sprawling!

STUFFUL ⬤ ⬡

Height: 1'08" / Weight: 15.0 lbs.
Type: Normal-Fighting
Category: Flailing Pokémon

BEWEAR ⬤ ⬡

Height: 6'11" / Weight: 297.6 lbs.
Type: Normal-Fighting
Category: Strong Arm Pokémon

Stufful evolves into the lumbering **Bewear**. Bewear's immense strength is well known throughout Alola, and its habitats are usually off-limits to prevent dangerous accidents!

SALANDIT 🌫️ 🔥

Height: 2'00" / Weight: 10.6 lbs.
Type: Poison-Fire
Category: Toxic Lizard Pokémon

Salandit makes its home near volcanoes and other warm, dry spots. It produces a gas that can poison any target, even Pokémon that are otherwise immune to poison!

ALOLAN MUK 🌫️ 🦷

Height: 3'03" / Weight: 114.6 lbs.
Type: Poison-Dark
Category: Sludge Pokémon

Unlike its counterparts in other regions, **Alolan Muk** is a vivid rainbow of colors, thanks to chemicals in the garbage it consumes. It is generally a good companion, but it can turn destructive when hungry.

ZUBAT

Height: 2'07" / **Weight:** 16.5 lbs.
Type: Poison-Flying
Category: Bat Pokémon

Zubat is a common Pokémon native to the Kanto region and found throughout Alola. Since it doesn't have eyes, Zubat emits ultrasonic waves to navigate its surroundings. Zubat colonies sleep in caves during the day.

CROBAT

Height: 5'11" / **Weight:** 165.3 lbs.
Type: Poison-Flying
Category: Bat Pokémon

Zubat evolves into Golbat, which then evolves into **Crobat**. Crobat has a second set of wings that allows it to quickly zoom through the air, making it a master of stealth and speed!

MUDBRAY

Height: 3'03" / Weight: 242.5 lbs.
Type: Ground
Category: Donkey Pokémon

Mudbray is a stubborn Ground-type Pokémon that likes to eat dirt and mess around in the mud all day. The mud packed on its hooves helps this Pokémon keep its grip when it runs.

MUDSDALE

Height: 8'02" / Weight: 2028.3 lbs.
Type: Ground
Category: Draft Horse Pokémon

Mudsdale is the evolved form of Mudbray. Mudsdale's powerful kicks can reduce a building to rubble, but many Alolans use the weather-resistant mud it produces to shore up their houses.

SANDYGAST 👻 ⛰️

Height: 1'08" / **Weight:** 154.3 lbs.
Type: Ghost-Ground
Category: Sand Heap Pokémon

Stories say that a child's sand castle on the beach became a **Sandygast**. Anyone who sticks a hand in its mouth may fall victim to its powerful mind control!

PALOSSAND 👻 ⛰️

Height: 4'03" / **Weight:** 551.2 lbs.
Type: Ghost-Ground
Category: Sand Castle Pokémon

Palossand is the evolved form of Sandygast. It lures people into its sandy depths and curses them. Be careful that you don't fall under the possession of this powerful Pokémon!

WOBBUFFET ◑

Height: 4'03" / Weight: 62.8 lbs.
Type: Psychic
Category: Patient Pokémon

Wobbuffet possesses high endurance and can withstand most attacks. Rather than wear itself out fighting, Wobbuffet does nothing but endure attacks—unless its foe goes after Wobbuffet's tail!

Meowth were brought to the Alola region by travelers, but thanks to human interference, their numbers swelled and they adapted to their new home. **Alolan Meowth** is a Dark-type Pokémon prone to furious rages if its precious gold Charm is smudged.

ALOLAN MEOWTH

Height: 1'04" / Weight: 9.3 lbs.
Type: Dark
Category: Scratch Cat Pokémon

ALOLAN RATICATE

Height: 2'04" / Weight: 56.2 lbs.
Type: Dark-Normal
Category: Mouse Pokémon

Alolan Raticate is the evolved form of Alolan Rattata and is known to gather a gang of Alolan Rattata to boss around. It is extremely picky about its food, so restaurants with Alolan Raticate infestations often earn a good reputation!

GRUBBIN 🦋

Height: 1'04" / Weight: 9.7 lbs.
Type: Bug
Category: Larva Pokémon

Grubbin's strong jaws allow it to slurp sap out of trees. Grubbin are known to gather near Electric-type Pokémon to hide from Flying-type Pokémon like Pikipek.

VIKAVOLT 🦋 ⚡

Height: 4'11" / Weight: 99.2 lbs.
Type: Bug-Electric
Category: Stag Beetle Pokémon

Vikavolt evolves from Charjabug, which is the evolved form of Grubbin. Vikavolt produces electricity in its body. Its massive jaws allow it to focus electrical energy to shock its foes!

LEDYBA 🦋 🌙

Height: 3'03" / Weight: 23.8 lbs.
Type: Bug-Flying
Category: Five Star Pokémon

Ledyba is a shy Pokémon that prefers to huddle with others of its kind. It was first discovered in the Johto region and can be found throughout Alola as well. They can communicate via scent—for instance, a swarm of angry Ledyba smells really sour!

LEDIAN 🦋 🌙

Height: 4'07" / Weight: 78.5 lbs.
Type: Bug-Flying
Category: Five Star Pokémon

Ledyba evolves into **Ledian**. It feeds on berries and absorbs energy from starlight. It tries to overwhelm foes by using all four of its fists at once.

SUDOWOODO ⬡

Height: 3'11" / **Weight:** 83.8 lbs.
Type: Rock
Category: Imitation Pokémon

Sudowoodo may look like a Grass-type Pokémon, but that's merely an illusion! This Rock-type Pokémon mimics trees to avoid danger. While Sudowoodo can stand very still, splashing it with water will make it run off—or attack!

ROCKRUFF ⬡

Height: 1'08" / **Weight:** 20.3 lbs.
Type: Rock
Category: Puppy Pokémon

Rockruff is the Puppy Pokémon. Because of its friendly demeanor and long history living alongside people, Rockruff is considered a perfect companion for newer Trainers, although its attitude gets tougher as it grows up.

Lycanroc is the evolved form of Rockruff. Its Midday Form is known to be a trustworthy partner if paired with a Trainer who raises it well. Lycanroc attacks with the sharp rocks in its mane.

LYCANROC ⬡

(MIDDAY FORM)
Height: 2'07" / Weight: 55.1 lbs.
Type: Rock
Category: Wolf Pokémon

LYCANROC ⬡

(MIDNIGHT FORM)
Height: 3'07" / Weight: 55.1 lbs.
Type: Rock
Category: Wolf Pokémon

Lycanroc's Midnight Form is much more reckless and hurls itself at its enemies with no concern for its own safety. It prefers to attack with crushingly powerful headbutts.

MIMIKYU

Height: 0'08" / **Weight:** 1.5 lbs.
Type: Ghost-Fairy
Category: Disguise Pokémon

Don't look! **Mimikyu** just wants to be liked by people and other Pokémon, which is why it hides its terrifying true form under a dingy old rag. No one knows its true form. If you befriend a lonely Mimikyu, be sure not to peek at what's under its disguise!

GASTLY

Height: 4'03" / **Weight:** 0.2 lbs.
Type: Ghost-Poison
Category: Gas Pokémon

Gastly is a Ghost- and Poison-type Pokémon first seen in the Kanto region. Gastly is often difficult to see, and its presence causes lights to flicker. It loves to play pranks on humans!

HAUNTER 👻 👻

Height: 5'03" / **Weight:** 0.2 lbs.
Type: Ghost-Poison
Category: Gas Pokémon

Gastly evolves into **Haunter**. Haunter strikes at its foes from the shadows, using its large tongue to send shivers up its opponent's spine—and drain its life force! Haunter may be on the verge of extinction in well-lit cities due to its fear of the light, so it prefers to stay in shadows.

GENGAR 👻 👻

Height: 4'11" / **Weight:** 89.3 lbs.
Type: Ghost-Poison
Category: Shadow Pokémon

If you ever feel a sudden chill, watch out—it might be an approaching **Gengar**! Gengar is the evolved form of Haunter. This Pokémon is said to be able to Mega Evolve into the terrifying Mega Gengar!

DRAMPA

Height: 9'10" / **Weight:** 407.9 lbs.
Type: Normal-Dragon
Category: Placid Pokémon

Drampa is a calm, compassionate Pokémon that makes its home deep within mountains far away. It is known to travel into towns to play with friendly children, but it can become extremely dangerous when angered.

DRAGONITE

Height: 7'03" / **Weight:** 463.0 lbs.
Type: Dragon-Flying
Category: Dragon Pokémon

Dragonite evolves from Dragonair, which evolves from Dratini, a Pokémon first found in the Kanto region. For many years, Dragonite was thought to be a mere legend. Even though this Pokémon possesses a calm demeanor, an angry Dragonite won't hesitate to unleash mighty attacks!

GOOMY

Height: 1'00" / Weight: 6.2 lbs.
Type: Dragon
Category: Soft Tissue Pokémon

Even though it's a Dragon-type Pokémon, **Goomy** is a very weak example of this generally powerful type. The slime that covers its body protects it.

GOODRA

Height: 6'07" / Weight: 331.8 lbs.
Type: Dragon
Category: Dragon Pokémon

Goomy evolves into Sliggoo, which evolves into **Goodra**, an amazingly friendly—and amazingly sticky—Pokémon. Goodra loves making friends and will often cry if left alone. It sometimes gets picked on by bullies—but a quick blow from its mighty horns and tail puts that to rest!

COMFEY 🍃

Height: 0'04" / **Weight:** 0.7 lbs.
Type: Fairy
Category: Posy Picker Pokémon

Comfey is a tiny Fairy-type Pokémon that gathers sweet-smelling flowers on its vine. Humans often collect the flowers to freshen up their baths, because Comfey's flowers have a calming fragrance.

CUTIEFLY 🦋 🍃

Height: 0'04" / **Weight:** 0.4 lbs.
Type: Bug-Fairy
Category: Bee Fly Pokémon

Cutiefly is said to sense auras and often swarms around good-natured people and flowers that are about to bloom. This Pokémon always knows where to find fresh nectar. If a group of Cutiefly are following you, you might have a floral aura!

KLEFKI ⬡ 〉

Height: 0'08" / **Weight:** 6.6 lbs.
Type: Steel-Fairy
Category: Key Ring Pokémon

Klefki is known for sneaking into homes and stealing keys—it loves to collect keys! The jangling of its keys may make Klefki seem cute and harmless, but its dual Steel and Fairy types makes it a menace to Dragon-type Pokémon!

METAGROSS ⬡ ◑

Height: 5'03" / **Weight:** 1212.5 lbs.
Type: Steel-Psychic
Category: Iron Leg Pokémon

Said to be the result of two Metang fusing together, **Metagross** can perform complex calculations in an instant with its four brains and pin its foes down with its four heavy arms. This Pokémon is said to be able to Mega Evolve into Mega Metagross.

SOLGALEO ◈ ⬡

Height: 11'02" / **Weight:** 507.1 lbs.
Type: Psychic-Steel
Category: Sunne Pokémon

Solgaleo and Lunala are majestic and powerful Legendary Pokémon of the Alola region and may have come from another world. Solgaleo radiates intense light from its metallic body and can illuminate the darkest nights.

LUNALA ◉ ☾

Height: 13'01" / **Weight:** 264.6 lbs.
Type: Psychic-Ghost
Category: Moone Pokémon

Lunala is said to devour light, pulling the shade of darkness over the brightest days. Both Legendary Pokémon have a third eye that, when activated, allows them to return to the world they make their homes in.

The tropical islands of Alola are full of even more new Pokémon to discover and Train. Have fun meeting new Pokémon and tough Trainers and exploring this exciting new region and beyond into the wider world of Pokémon!

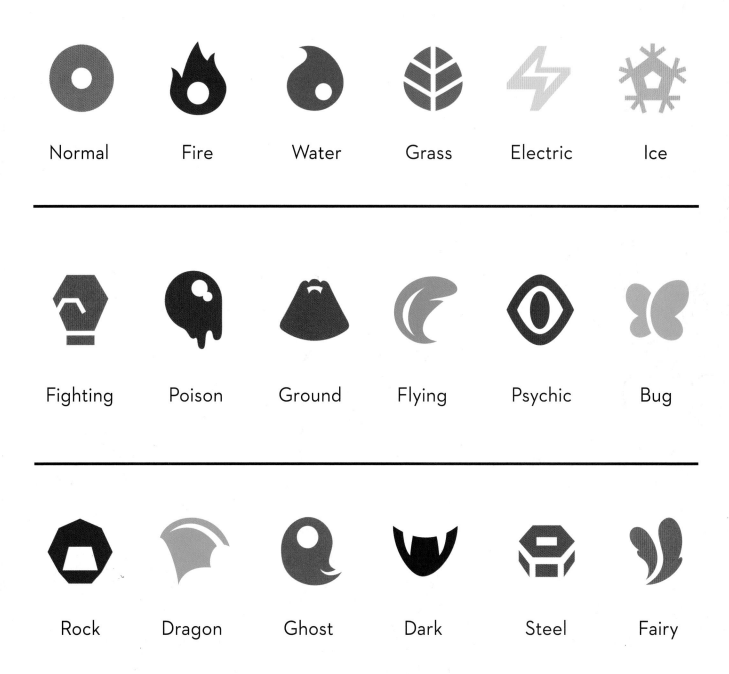

| Normal | Fire | Water | Grass | Electric | Ice |

| Fighting | Poison | Ground | Flying | Psychic | Bug |

| Rock | Dragon | Ghost | Dark | Steel | Fairy |